"I loved the book and I learned something new from every page!!!" —Emily

"*My Name Is Erin: One Girl's Mission to Make a Difference* has taught me how I can make a difference in the world even at my age. By reading this book I've learned to take the eyes off myself and put them in places that really matter. It has practical ideas that answer the questions we all think about in our everyday lives. Every teen girl struggles with theses things and should read this book!"—Hannah

my name is

ERIN

One Girl's Mission to
Make a Difference

Erin Davis

MOODY PUBLISHERS
CHICAGO

© 2013 by
ERIN DAVIS

All Scripture quotations, unless otherwise indicated, are taken from *The Holy Bible, English Standard Version.* Copyright © 2000, 2001 by Crossway Bibles, a division of Good News Publishers. Used by permission. All rights reserved.

Scripture quotations marked ASV are taken from *The American Standard Version,* 1901, public domain.

Scripture quotations marked NIV are taken from the Holy Bible, New International Version®, NIV®. Copyright © 1973, 1978, 1984 by Biblica, Inc.™ Used by permission of Zondervan. All rights reserved worldwide. www.zondervan.com

All websites and phone numbers listed herein are accurate at the time of publication, but may change in the future or cease to exist. The listing of website references and resources does not imply publisher endorsement of the site's entire contents. Groups and organizations are listed for informational purposes, and listing does not imply publisher endorsement of their activities.

Edited by Annette LaPlaca
Interior and Cover design: Julia Ryan / www.DesignByJulia.com
Cover images: Shutterstock/Elise Gravel. Illustration of author: Julia Ryan
Interior images: Various artists/Shutterstock: frames, borders, butterfly, arrows, flowers, faces, pencil, pen, decorative art, bullhorn, bee, sun, words, bus, earphones. Chapter illustration: Beastfromeast/iStock
Author photo: Sarah Carter Photography

Library of Congress Cataloging-in-Publication Data

Davis, Erin, 1980-
 My name is Erin : one girl's mission to make a difference / Erin Davis.
  pages cm
 Includes bibliographical references.
 ISBN 978-0-8024-0644-6
1. Vocation--Christianity--Juvenile literature. 2. Preteens--Religious life--Juvenile literature. 3. Teenage girls--Religious life--Juvenile literature. 4. Davis, Erin, 1980---Juvenile literature. I. Title.
 BV4740.D345 2013
 248.8'33--dc23

                                  2013013038

We hope you enjoy this book from Moody Publishers. Our goal is to provide high-quality, thought-provoking books and products that connect truth to your real needs and challenges. For more information on other books and products written and produced from a biblical perspective, go to www.moodypublishers.com or write to:

Moody Publishers
820 N. LaSalle Boulevard
Chicago, IL 60610

1 3 5 7 9 10 8 6 4 2

Printed in the United States of America

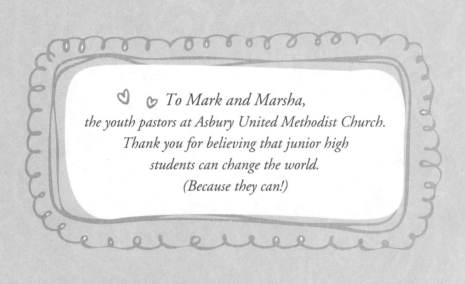

*To Mark and Marsha,
the youth pastors at Asbury United Methodist Church.
Thank you for believing that junior high
students can change the world.
(Because they can!)*

Contents

CHAPTER 1

Your Mission
(Should You Choose to Accept It)

My name is Erin. I'm a Milk Dud–loving momma who is passionate about a few things, including (in no particular order) my family, the perfect scoop of ice cream, God's Word, a simple life on my little farm, and teaching young women to choose God's Truth.

I bet you're a passionate girl too. Maybe you share my love for farm living and own a horse or two. Maybe you're a writer like me, who gets jazzed about words, stories, and blog posts. Maybe you are especially passionate about children or there's a corner of the world that tugs at your heartstrings. Perhaps you are passionate about a certain band or sports team, fashion, or a well-brewed caramel latte. No matter who you are or where you live, I'm sure there are things that cause your pulse to race and your heart to go pitter-patter.

Some of our passions are simply a byproduct of our environment. We love what our parents love; we get jazzed about whatever makes our friends tick. But I have a theory that there are other passions, the ones that ooze from our very core, that have been woven into our hearts by a passionate God with a passionate plan to take the world by storm. Okay, it's not really my theory. God outlines our mission clearly in His Word. We'll get to that soon.

How can we know which passions are God-given? What should we do with those passions? Should we bridle them or let them run free, giving them reign over the way we live our lives and the choices we make for the future? Is passion a fire we should seek to control or something we should let consume our entire lives?

These are questions I've tried to wrestle to the ground since I was a little girl. (That's me in the fourth grade.)

Like a Chihuahua on a leash, I've bounced back and forth from place to place seeking to find my passion and then wondering what do next. I want to be turned loose with the things that most excite me, but I feel gently pulled back by a God who seems to desire to direct my passions for use in His bigger story.

Speaking of God, why did He make me? What is my purpose on this planet? Do my passions have anything to do with that?

These questions won't win me any awards for originality. People in every culture in every age have wondered, "What am I here for?" As one of billions of people on one planet in one solar system in one of many galaxies, I naturally search for significance. Self-help books tell us to find the answer within ourselves, but those books miss something huge—the God who created us. His Word says that we were created on purpose.

Isaiah 43:7 talks about His people: "Everyone who is called by my name, whom I created for my glory, whom I formed and made."

Read that passage backward. You were made and formed by God. Why? For His glory. Your purpose on this planet is tied to the God who made you. God and your purpose in life cannot be separated.

With that in mind, is God's heart the best place to take our passions? Is He in charge of deciding our purpose? Will He show us what it looks like to be created for His glory?

I've opened the Bible and asked God to answer these questions and to show me my purpose. I've squeezed my passions through the grid of God's Word. The result is a plan to live *on mission*, finding my purpose in using my God-given passions to do kingdom work.

Check out these hilarious titles of real self-help books:

The Zombie Survival Guide: Complete Protection from the Living Dead

Things I've Learned from Women Who've Dumped Me

Faking It: How to Seem Like a Better Person without Actually Improving Yourself

 My name is Erin and this is my story.

Your Mission (Should You Choose to Accept It)

God has a purpose for your life.

That may sound like a cheesy bumper sticker or a mushy Hallmark card, but that single sentence can radically change your life. You are not an accident. Your life is not a series of coincidences strung together between birth and death. Nope. God has a mission for you. And much like the famous spy in *Mission Impossible*, you have the choice to accept your mission or simply let it self-destruct.

From here on out, you'll read the phrase "living on mission" a lot. Sounds like more spy talk! What does it mean? Living on mission is living on purpose. It is the opposite of floating through life, finding meaning here and there. Living on mission means building a life based on a goal. We will dig up the specifics of that goal in the chapters of this book, but for now, living on mission simply means to do what God made you to do.

Since no mission-minded girl should ever face the world alone, let me introduce you to some girls I know you're gonna love. Before I started writing this book, some friends and I traveled the nation interviewing

There's an app for self-destructing messages. Software makers have developed a free iPhone app that sends messages that delete themselves within seconds. Now you see it. Now you don't.

girls just like you about what it means to live life on a mission. We went to big cities and small towns and everywhere in between. The girls we talked to had been exposed to plenty of Christian talk. They know how to talk the talk about God and purpose. (I call that speaking Christianese.) The girls went to different schools and had different interests, but they had something in common: They wanted their lives to matter. They longed to be a part of something bigger than themselves. But they weren't quite there . . . yet.

They also loved to talk. That's why I've nicknamed them the Gab Gallery. From here on out, I'll just call them the Gallery. You'll hear their stories and read their thoughts throughout the pages of this book. Their role is to make you feel like you are part of a conversation about finding purpose (because you are!).

The Gallery Girls!

The Gallery girls loved talking about purpose. Of all the subjects we covered with them, purpose got them the most excited (then they really started talking). In fact, these were girls with passions for big causes like Kids Against Hunger, Compassion International, and Invisible Children.

13

We're not talking about lemonade stands and helping little old ladies across the street here! These girls saw the value in causes that influenced millions of lives. And yet, everywhere we went, there was a gap between the Gallery girls' passions and living their lives with a mission in mind. These girls were passionate, but they had a sideline mentality. "I will cheer you on" was their general attitude about anything big that was happening for the kingdom.

"Grown-ups are given all the credit if I do something big," they said.

"It's assumed that adults are just more sophisticated and smarter. They assume that we won't understand," they said when pressed about why they aren't living on mission now.

The Gallery girls said they wanted to live their lives on mission, but there was this sense that living on mission was something they would do later and that God had big plans for them "someday." They thought that mission-minded living was for people with college degrees, fancy jobs, and fat bank accounts. Sure, they prayed and read their Bibles, but putting their faith into action was for later. They knew a lot about God's Word, but they didn't yet base their decisions on God's Truth.

Find out more about the Gallery girls' passions on these websites:
kidsagainsthunger.org
Compassion.com
invisiblechildren.com
girlscouts.org

🌼 Hello. It's God Calling.

I became a Christian when I was fifteen. From then on, I was fascinated by people who did big things with their faith. I told anyone who would listen to me that God was going to use me to do something important too, but I didn't have a clue what that would look like. I admired missionaries who sold everything to reach needy people in faraway lands. I adored pastors who passionately preached God's Word to the masses. I loved the Mother Teresas and Billy Grahams who did radical things for the kingdom. The giants of the faith often talked about feeling "called." It was as if God sent an assignment directly to their smartphone, and they answered, "Yes, Lord!" Now, that's living on mission!

But me? I had math homework. I had a curfew. I had parents who seemed more interested in how clean my bedroom was than if I was living out my God-given purpose. From the very moment I became a Christian, I wanted to do big things for God, yet what was my purpose exactly? How could I live on mission when I was still so young?

And so I waited. I waited for tools I did not need and missed out on an exciting mission that only required obedience to God and His Word.

If I had a time machine, I'd go back and do things differently.

I don't have a time machine, but maybe I don't need one. This book isn't just about me. It's a chance to rewrite the pages of your own story, a chance to take it from an average tale to the kind of epic adventure that only gets written about girls who live their lives for something bigger than themselves. It doesn't matter how old you are. It doesn't matter if you've got a stack of homework to do. It doesn't matter if you're on the volleyball team, the honor roll, or the list of who's most likely to succeed.

 God's got a purpose for your life. You are called to do important things just like the people who seem like giants of the faith. The question is, will you shift your thinking toward God's view of purpose? Will you let Him shape your passions into a mission for His glory?

There's that word again—*passion*. I know we just met, but I'm going to make a prediction. I bet there is a connection between what you're passionate about and the mission God wants to call you to. Or maybe God has set a passion deep inside your heart. It's lying there dormant, waiting for you to seek God's plan for the way you live your life from this point forward.

With that in mind, we will use passion as a starting point. In the space below write down the things you are most passionate about. Now, don't speak Christianese. Don't write down a churchy answer that you think might impress your Sunday school teacher (I doubt she will be reading your list). Get real about what really excites you. If you don't have a passion yet, that's okay. God wants to show you His passion in the pages of His Word, and it's contagious. It won't be long until you've got something really cool to be passionate about.

I am passionate about:

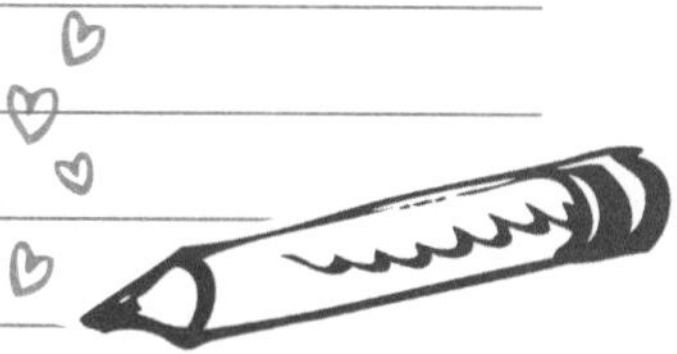

_____

_____

_____

_____

_____

_____

_____

That list is just a beginning, a springboard to send us off in search of our purpose. Before we launch too high, we'd better take a minute to check in with mission control.

So put down your book for a minute and ask God to use this book to show you His purpose for your life. Your prayer might sound something like this: "God, thank You for creating me to bring glory to You. I'm not sure exactly what that means, but I want my life to matter. I want You to use me to do something big. Would You show me my purpose through Your Word?"

CHAPTER 2

Putting a
Leash on My
Chihuahua
Mentality

f you read *My Name Is Erin: One Girl's Journey to Discover Who She Is* from this series, you know that I consider myself a bulldog. I wrote, "While my twin sister was playing house, I was pretending to be the boss. Other girls are so naturally sweet that they come across like little cocker spaniels. I've always been a bit more like a bulldog."[1]

I still think I'd make a pretty good bulldog.

But I can also be a dead ringer for a Chihuahua sometimes too. Chihuahuas are feisty little dogs known for barking often and jumping everywhere.

If you put a Chihuahua on a leash, he's not likely to walk calmly beside you like my Goldendoodle, Marley (good boy)! Most Chihuahuas would yank and pull and dart and struggle against that leash. It's as if they are looking for validation here and there to make up for the fact that they are lacking in size and beauty.

Did you know that this book is just one in a four-book series? Check out the other My Name Is Erin books at erindavis.org.

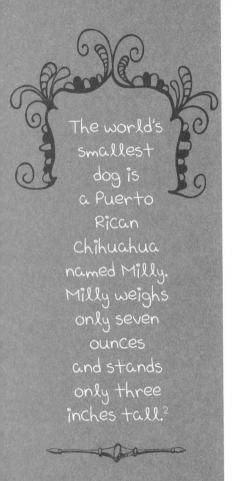

The world's smallest dog is a Puerto Rican Chihuahua named Milly. Milly weighs only seven ounces and stands only three inches tall.[2]

Chihuahua lovers, please do not send me hate mail. I am sure your pup is fabulous! And if imitation is the highest form of flattery, then I must be a fan because I've spent much of my life acting like a Chihuahua. Let me explain.

I have a twin sister who was born one minute before I was (a mere technicality), but I have all of the characteristics of a firstborn. I am strong-willed. I am driven. I love to achieve. I'm a hard worker who craves hearing "Atta girl!" Compliments are like a choice dessert to me. Mmmm, it's yummy when someone notices I've done something well.

That craving for affirmation and achievement has often sent me sniffing for purpose. In junior high, my search for purpose made me try to be the very best student in every class. Getting a B would throw me into a total meltdown. I had my beady eyes focused on a singular mission: to get good grades, which would lead to a good college, which would almost certainly score me an important job.

Fast-forward to high school. I still wanted to get good grades, but I was sniffing down a different purpose by then. I wanted to be popular. I wanted people to like me. In fact, I wanted everyone to like me. I wanted them to like me more than they liked any other girl in school. Surely if I had my own fan club that would give me purpose.

Jump ahead to college. I was determined to find purpose in the perfect career. Suddenly I was sniffing a trail that smelled a lot like a combination of my junior high and high school mentalities. I wanted to achieve a lot, and I wanted people to notice. I ended up majoring in public relations, basically studying how to make people and companies look good. I wasn't particularly passionate about it, but I thought having a career that made good money and allowed me to climb the corporate ladder would give my life meaning.

I also developed an eating disorder in college. I became obsessed with being thin. I yanked on the leash God wanted to use to direct me toward His purposes for me and tried to make myself matter by being prettier, thinner, and more attractive than the other girls around me. I became like a dog sticking his nose in a snake hole because that particular search for significance bit me back. The eating disorder took a toll on my heart and body, and it was ugly.

There are other things I have chased through the years in an attempt to find purpose. Sometimes it was closer friends or more stuff or a pet project. Sometimes it's even been spirituality. I'd convince myself that if I would just read my Bible more or pray more or get more involved in church, surely that would give my life meaning.

As I look back, I see I was trying to drink from very shallow wells. It's not that I was necessarily looking for purpose in "bad" things; it's just that nothing I chased down could give me purpose that lasted long. There was no significant mission I could focus on through the changing seasons of life.

When we look for purpose here and there, we shouldn't be surprised when the results feel empty. God warns us in the Bible that this will happen. I want you to drink from deep wells, girls! I want you to avoid my mistakes by finding purpose in what really matters.

With that in mind, let's approach my story like a science-class experiment. We'll dissect it and study it to see what we can learn.

First, let's examine my heart. I was specifically looking for purpose in:

* Achievement
* Beauty
* Affirmation

I am sure there are one or two things on that list that you look to in order to give your life purpose. Maybe you've chased after all of them at one time or another. But, like me, I bet you've found them to be shallow wells.

You cannot fill yourself up with them. You cannot make yourself matter with them. Let's take that list to the textbook of God's Word to find out why.

🌸 Achievement

Achievement means to earn through your effort. It's not exactly the same as hard work. God actually applauds hard work in verses like Colossians 3:23 and Proverbs 13:4. As Christians we should work hard at everything we do as a way to show the world we want to put our best foot forward. The problem comes when we look to our hard work to give our lives meaning.

Many scholars believe the Old Testament book of Ecclesiastes was written by King Solomon. Solomon achieved plenty. He built God's temple and a personal palace, captured foreign lands, secured his kingdom, grew and fortified cities, and collected lots and lots of gold (2 Chronicles 8). Yet all of that effort didn't give Solomon lasting purpose.

Solomon wrapped up Ecclesiastes this way: "The end of the matter; all has been heard. Fear God and keep his commandments, for this is the whole duty of man" (Ecclesiastes 12:13).

Solomon boils down our mission to just two tasks:

1. Fear God   2. Keep His commandments

If Solomon were a student, he would have been valedictorian. If he were an athlete, he would have won an Olympic gold medal. He knew what it was like to achieve. But at the end of the day, Solomon realized he couldn't work his way into a life that mattered. His words show us our own purpose.

Achieving goals is fine. God wants you to work hard, and yet getting good grades and winning awards is not why God created you. Remember, you were made to bring God glory. You can do that by fearing Him and living like His Word tells you to.

Fearing God doesn't mean being afraid of Him. It means having a healthy respect for Him and a right understanding that He is God and you are not. It means submitting your life to Him because you recognize that His ways are best.

Affirmation

Girls seem especially fond of compliments. I'm sure guys like compliments too, but we crave them, don't we? We really, really, really want people to notice us and tell us what they like about us.

But Luke 6:26 warns, "Woe to you, when all people speak well of you." Jesus was telling His disciples to watch out for the dangers of seeking the approval of the people around them.

It's not that compliments are bad. We shouldn't try to avoid them or argue with people when they say nice things. (That's called false modesty.) But we get into trouble when we decide whether or not we matter based on what other people think. It's dangerous to find personal purpose in pleasing others because then we will do whatever it takes to keep the compliments coming.

Have you ever thought, "Whew! I got a lot of compliments today. I don't need another word of affirmation for a week." Nope. It doesn't work that way. The more compliments we get, the more compliments we crave.

Affirmation is a shallow well, because it's like pouring water into a bucket with a hole in it. We can never, ever get filled up by the praise of others.

John 12:43 describes the Pharisees this way: "For they loved human praise more than praise from God" (NIV).

The Bible says that it was the Pharisees' craving for human praise that kept them from recognizing that Jesus was the Savior (John 12:40–41). That's the danger in trying to find our purpose in what others think. It causes us to chase after whatever will get us praised instead of recognizing what God wants us to do.

❀ Beauty

Through the years my struggle to find purpose through my beauty has been intense. I've chased down lies like "If I

The Pharisees were religious leaders in Jesus' day. They loved to add things to the Word of God and to follow the Bible to the letter to prove how spiritual they were. Jesus was always calling them out because their hearts were self-focused instead of focused on God and others. ♡

were only thinner, then I would matter" or "If I just had new clothes, that would give me value," but it never works. I lose the weight, but it doesn't give my life meaning. I buy new clothes, but it doesn't give me any lasting sense of purpose.

Proverbs 31:30 holds the key to the reason why the pursuit of physical beauty doesn't work to provide purpose: "Charm is deceptive, and beauty is fleeting, but a woman who fears the Lord is to be praised" (NIV).

Feeling ugly?

Check out some of these bizarre beauty rituals from around the world, and I'm sure you'll decide what you see in the mirror is A-Ok!

 In Israel, women get massages from slithering snakes.

 In Turkey, women soak their tootsies in a tub of water full of fish before a pedicure. The fish are supposed to nibble away at dead skin.

 In Chile, snail secretions are harvested and put into beauty creams because they are thought to produce exceptionally smooth skin.[3]

Beauty is deceptive. It's tricky. It doesn't last.
Looking for purpose in outward beauty is impossible, because no beauty cream or exercise routine can preserve our outward beauty forever. A lifetime spent trying to matter by chasing outward beauty is a waste. Clear skin, great hair, and a tiny jeans size can't compare to the thrill of living for something bigger than ourselves.

As we yank this way and that way looking for our mission, we can start to feel exhausted. God doesn't want us to drink from a shallow well. There is another way.

Drinking from a well reminds me of an encounter Jesus had with a Samaritan woman. The story is told in John 4:7–15.

> A woman from Samaria came to draw water. Jesus said to her, "Give me a drink." (For his disciples had gone away into the city to buy food.) The Samaritan woman said to him, "How is it that you, a Jew, ask for a drink from me, a woman of Samaria?" (For Jews have no dealings with Samaritans.) Jesus answered her, "If you knew the gift of God, and who it is that is saying to you, 'Give me a drink,' you would have asked him, and he would have given you living water." The woman said to him, "Sir, you have nothing to draw water with, and the well is deep. Where do you get that living water? Are you greater than our father Jacob? He gave us the well and drank from

it himself, as did his sons and his livestock." Jesus said to her, "Everyone who drinks of this water will be thirsty again, but whoever drinks of the water that I will give him will never be thirsty again. The water that I will give him will become in him a spring of water welling up to eternal life."

Jesus is a deep well. He offers us living water, the kind that can finally quench our thirst for purpose.

When we find our purpose in Him and what He wants for our lives, we stop looking for purpose everywhere else. God alone is able to give us a mission that lasts.

Christ's purpose for me reminds me of a song we sing at my church. The lyrics say, "I am free to run. I am free to dance. I am free to live for You. I am free." There is freedom in living our lives for Christ. There is freedom in accepting His mission to focus our lives on glorifying Him.

What does that kind of mission feel like?

Like a dog . . . running without a leash . . . toward a deep well that will satisfy his thirst forever. Cool, huh?

I'm just the specimen here. The true goal is for you to discover if you've been living like a Chihuahua, trying to chase down purpose in shallow wells. So it's time to dissect your own heart.

Think for a minute about where you turn to find purpose. Here are a few questions to help you think it through.

1. What makes me feel great about myself?

 2. What are the three goals that are most important for me to achieve?

 3. Before I read this chapter, if someone asked me to describe my purpose in one word, what would I have said?

 4. Where have I looked for purpose but found it was a shallow well?

Setting Things Straight

The bottom line is that anything you pursue in order to make your life matter, apart from God, will miss that mark.

The bottom line is that anything you pursue in order to make your life matter, apart from God, will miss that mark.

No, that wasn't a typo. I wanted you to read that sentence twice so it would sink deep into your hearts.

When we recognize that God created us and gives us purpose and that He alone can give us a mission that matters, we are free to stop chasing after satisfaction in shallow wells.

❀ The One Thing

Have you ever heard the story of Mary and Martha? It's a tale of two sisters found in Luke 10:38–42. Here's the Erin paraphrase.

Martha was a Chihuahua. I'd say she got specifically worked up about finding purpose in achievement and affirmation. One day Jesus came to her house and Martha worked herself into a total tizzy. She cleaned every square inch. She whipped up a feast. She probably even ironed the napkins.

And then . . . she waited.

She waited for Jesus to notice and compliment her on everything she had done.

But He didn't. He was busy spending time with Martha's sister, Mary, who did nothing more than sit at Jesus' feet.

For real. The Bible tells us that while Martha was working her fingers to the bone, Mary wasn't exerting any effort at all. She was just sitting there. What kind of mission is that?

Notice what Jesus said to Martha when she got bent out of shape from the discovery that achievement and affirmation were shallow wells: "Martha, Martha, you are anxious and troubled about many things, but one thing is necessary. Mary has chosen the good portion, which will not be taken away from her" (Luke 10:41–42).

Martha yanked herself this way and that way trying to find meaning, but Jesus said she only needed one thing.

One. As in greater than zero, but less than two. Not many. Not a few. Jesus said that only one thing was necessary.

What was the one thing? It was Him. It was Jesus. Being with Him should have been Martha's singular mission that day. Anything else she turned to for meaning was doomed to fade away into meaninglessness.

Mary knew what her mission was, and so she sat. She didn't strive. She didn't obsess over who thought what about her. I'm not even sure if she checked her reflection in the mirror. She sat with Jesus because He matters most. Her obedience may not have earned her any medals or achievement awards, but she did earn a reward that could never be taken from her.

Are you a Mary or a Martha? Do you live your life on mission for the one thing that matters, or are you looking for purpose all over the place?

We've already looked at the essence of your mission in Isaiah 43:7. Here it is again. "Everyone who is called by my name, whom I created for my glory, whom I formed and made."

You were made for God's glory. That means your purpose is to make God famous. You can bring God glory in big things and in the small stuff. That might look like being a great athlete who acknowledges that your talent comes from God instead of looking to score attention for yourself. It might mean working toward a future career that matches up with the heartbeat of God spelled out in His Word. It might mean saying no to some things because you need to take more time to simply sit with Jesus.

Get in the habit of asking yourself, "Does this glorify God?" That one question will help you accomplish your God-given mission one step at a time.

God gives us other missions in His Word.

Remember Ecclesiastes 12:13? Part of your mission is to fear God and to keep His commandments. How would it change things if you considered obeying God's commandments your new mission in life?

> To accomplish your mission one step at a time, get in the habit of asking yourself, "Does this glorify God?"

Philippians 3:9–10 urges us to know Christ and to be found in Him. It is part of your mission in life to get to know God. You do this by reading His Word often, by talking to Him through prayer, and by spending time with Christians who know God and can teach you more about Him.

Matthew 28:19 tells how Jesus gave His followers "the Great Commission." He doesn't use those words to tell us to achieve, or to look like supermodels, or to make sure people like us. Instead He says, "Go therefore and make disciples of all nations, baptizing them in the name of the Father and of the Son and of the Holy Spirit."

Your mission is to go and to tell others about what Jesus has done.

You don't have to wonder about your purpose in life. The Bible is very clear.

Your mission (should you choose to accept it) is to:

★ Make God famous
★ Fear God
★ Keep God's commandments
★ Know Christ
★ Go! Tell others about Jesus

It's a short list but a tall order. It's not an easy mission to live out, and you won't do it perfectly, but it sure beats looking for purpose here and there and coming up empty. To agree to live *on mission* is to sign up for a God-sized adventure with results that cannot be taken from you. That means they last forever!

God wants to use you in His huge story. He created you because you have a role to play. Understanding that key Truth opens you up to an adventure bigger than you've ever imagined.

CHAPTER 3

Waiting on
Mission
control

here are parts of the mission that all of us are called to as Christ-followers. These are the things we just looked at in God's Word. But just in case you are a slow learner (like me) when it comes to living out our God-given mission, here is a recap.

★ You were created to . . . make God famous.

★ Your purpose is to . . . fear God.

★ Your goal should be to . . . keep God's commandments.

★ You were designed to . . . know Christ.

★ Your assignment is to . . . tell others about Jesus.

That's the big picture, but are there other, smaller missions that aren't for everyone? Does God sometimes call one individual to one specific mission for one particular season? The Bible shows us that the clear answer is yes! Some of the biggest heroes of the Bible are individuals who heard the voice of God assign them a specific task or mission, and they responded with a version of "Yes, Lord!"

We'll explore a few of those stories in this chapter. As we do, I want you to pay close attention to what these men and women were doing when they heard the call of God and how they responded once they received their marching orders.

A Mission from a Burning Bush

The story of Moses may be familiar to you. It's a story we usually learn as kids at church or pretty soon after we start following Christ. You may already know all about Moses telling Pharaoh to "Let my people go," or that God parted the waters of the Red Sea when Moses held up his staff. Perhaps you're familiar with the story of Moses coming down from Mount Sinai with ten commandments written into stone. (If not, be sure to read Exodus. It beats any script Hollywood could ever write!) Moses's story can become so familiar that we miss the wonder of it all. God chose Moses for a humongous mission, but why? What was it about Moses that made him the man to experience such a high dose of God's power and calling?

For that answer, we've got to head to the sheep fields.

Now Moses was keeping the flock of his father-in-law, Jethro, the priest of Midian, and he led his flock to the west side of the wilderness and came to Horeb, the mountain of God. And the angel of the Lord appeared to him in a flame of fire out of a bush. He looked, and behold, the bush was burning, yet it was not consumed. And Moses said, "I will turn aside to see this great sight, why the bush is not burned." When the Lord saw that he had turned aside to see, God called to him out of the bush. (Exodus 3:1–4)

God went on to assign Moses the very specific task of delivering the people of Israel from Egypt, where they were slaves.

What was Moses doing when God called him to this mission? Was he away at a spiritual retreat seeking to hear from the Lord? Was he enrolled in a prestigious Bible college studying how God works? Was he polishing up his resume?

♡ Nope. He was herding sheep.

We need a little backstory to know why this matters. Moses hadn't always been a sheepherder. Exodus 2 tells us that, while he was born to an Israelite mother, he was adopted by the daughter of the Pharaoh. That meant his adopted momma was an Egyptian. He grew up in a palace. He knew what it was like to have achievement, money, prestige, and attention. But notice that Moses was not in the position of having it all when God called him to a super-sized mission.

Moses wasn't training for anything important when God found him, at least not in the ways we think he would be getting ready to hear from God. Don't miss this. Training to be used by God is more likely to happen in the sheep fields than it is to happen in the palace. God isn't waiting for you to cross a bunch of achievements off a to-do list before He will use you. Being ready to be used by

Why did Moses leave the palace? Moses ran away from home after murdering an Egyptian and burying his body in the sand. I told you this was the stuff that movies are made of! Read the whole story in Exodus 2:11-22.

God isn't about knowing the Bible frontward and backward or being some kind of spiritual superhero who follows Jesus perfectly. To be used by God you don't have to have it all figured out or have access to endless time and money to make things happen. You just have to be watching for the presence of God and be willing to turn toward Him when He speaks.

There's another big takeaway we shouldn't miss about Moses's mission. He was passionate about his calling before God ever came a knocking.

Moses was the biological son of an Israelite and the adopted son of an Egyptian. He had a foot in both camps and there were likely people that he loved on both sides of the fence. He ran from Egypt as a young man, and probably when he had a free afternoon to daydream, his thoughts often returned to his sandy homeland.

Sometimes there is a connection between those things that tug hardest on our heartstrings and the mission God has for us. Not every passion is God-given and not every God-given mission is connected to what we daydream about, but sometimes it seems that our passions are like fuel, waiting to be ignited into something bigger by a mission-minded God.

Your passion button may hold a clue to the ways God wants to use you.

❀ A Mission for Mary

When we think of examples from the Bible of people who were called by God to do big things, Mary jumps off the page. Mary's mission was to mother the Son of God. How's that for huge? And yet like Moses, Mary wasn't chosen because she was the most qualified person for the job. In fact, she may have been the least qualified. She was young. She was unmarried. She didn't know how to be a mother.

And yet . . . "In the sixth month the angel Gabriel was sent from God to a city of Galilee named Nazareth, to a virgin betrothed to a man whose name was Joseph, of the house of David. And the virgin's name was Mary. And he came to her and said, 'Greetings, O favored one, the Lord is with you!'" (Luke 1:26–28).

The angel Gabriel went on to give the details of Mary's very specific assignment. She was going to have a baby. She should name him Jesus. She was given the supernatural secret that her son was also the Son of the Most High God.

We hear this story every Christmas. It makes sense to us because we know how the story ends, but to Mary? Surely she struggled to connect all of the dots in her head. She was supposed to have a baby even though she didn't yet have a husband? She was to carry the Son of God in her womb and then what? How do you raise the Son of God?

Mary may not have been herding sheep like Moses, but she wasn't looking for a God-sized mission either. She was living her life, making plans for her future, when God broke in with something . . . bigger.

We skipped the end of Moses's calling, but if you read Exodus 3–4, you'd find that after expressing some doubt, Moses eventually agreed to go and do what God called him to. Mary expressed some hesitation too, but ultimately she accepted the mission God had for her.

Luke 1:38 records, "And Mary said, 'Behold, I am the servant of the Lord; let it be to me according to your word.'"

"Yes, Lord!"

♥ Here's that in translation:

Mary and Moses show us that God doesn't only have callings for those who have it all or the ones who can do it all. He seems to be most interested in finding those who will answer, "Yes, Lord!" He's looking for those with a willing heart.

40

I've never heard God speak from a burning bush or had an encounter with the angel Gabriel, but I do know what it is like to feel God calling me to do something out of my comfort zone.

Several years ago I was working as a high school history teacher. (Don't groan. Cool history teachers do exist!) Seemingly out of nowhere I felt God asking me to quit my job and write to young women. At the time, God's timing didn't make sense to me. I didn't have publishers knocking down my door asking me to write for them. In fact, I had zero opportunities to write anything other than entries in my journal. Why should I write to no one? How would I pay the bills when no one was offering me a book deal? What if I didn't have anything interesting to say?

I faced a season of hesitation just like Moses and Mary, but eventually I landed on "Yes, Lord!" as my response to His calling.

It wasn't like the clouds parted, the birds started singing, and the writing gigs came floating in just because I agreed to let God use me. For eight long months I sat in a tiny office at home with no work, no direction, and no idea what to write about. I cried a lot during those days, but I continued to trust that God had a plan and that obeying Him was my ticket to a bigger story than I could write for myself. I just could not shake the feeling that God was calling me to write for His glory.

Eventually, I did get opportunities. This book can be traced back to those many months with no one to read what I didn't know how to write. It is one of the beautiful results of the fact that God was willing to use me, despite my many imperfections.

What else kept me going when I couldn't see the finish line? Passion. There's that word again. It's like I took a giant pepper shaker and sprinkled "passion" all over this book. That's because the first thing that will motivate us away from "normal" and into the kind of radical life that comes with living on mission is a passion for God. When we love Him with our whole heart, living the life He calls us to makes sense because we trust Him and desire to please Him. But sometimes God plants other passions into our hearts like tiny seeds. Then He waters them and nurtures them until they are ready to bloom into a God-sized mission.

If you read *My Name Is Erin: One Girl's Journey to Discover Truth*, the first book in this series, you know that the idea to write didn't just occur to me one day in my twenties.

"My whole life I've wanted to be a writer," I wrote. "My classmates listed aspirations like astronaut, veterinarian, and movie star as their future goals. Not me. From kindergarten until high school, I consistently dreamed of writing books. True, I did have a few misguided months in college where I thought I wanted to be a dental hygienist ("Open wide!"), but for the most part this book you are holding in your hands is the realization of a dream I've had since I was a little girl."[4]

Looking back I can see that writing words that matter is a passion God sowed into my life very early.

open wide!

Psalm 37:4 says, "Delight yourself in the Lord, and he will give you the desires of your heart."

For a long time, I misunderstood this verse. I thought it meant that if I chose to be delighted by God, He would give me the things I want. Perhaps if I really, really liked God, He'd give me my dream job, my dream house, or lots of friends. But now I don't think this passage means that when we love God, He will give us what we want.

Now I realize this passage means that when we love God, He will change what we want. He gives us new desires. He changes our hearts so we want what *He* wants.

Writing about God's Truth to young women is a God-given desire for me. Sometimes my passion to see girls like you transformed by God's Truth burns so hot, I worry it will sear me. I can't *not* write to you about what God is teaching me. The more I delight in Him and His Word, the more He changes my desires to want to pass on the flame to you so that you can have all that you need to choose Truth.

As you seek to live on mission for God, you can know you are on the right path if your passions line up with His.

There have been other times when I have felt God calling me to something specific. Sometimes God is prompting me to do some little thing, like calling up a certain friend with a word of encouragement or praying for someone whose name God lays on my heart. Sometimes God calls me to big things. There was a season in my life when I knew God was calling me to become a mother. Embracing that calling scared the hooey out of me! But I said, "Yes, Lord." Today, being a mom is my very favorite job. As a family, we recently felt the Lord was calling us to move to a new town where the ministry need is great. Not being a huge fan of boxes, moving vans, and saying goodbye to friends, I wanted to resist. But I've learned from experience the kind of rewards that can only come from saying, "Yes, Lord" when He calls me to change direction. So we packed up the U-Haul and drove off to a whole new life.

🌼 God Waiting for God

I asked you to pay attention to what Moses and Mary were doing before they heard their assignment from God. Moses was in the desert, herding sheep. Mary was simply living life. Moses and Mary didn't try to force God to use them. They didn't try to drum up a calling or twist God's arm to use them for something big. They show us there is a difference between receiving God's calling and taking matters into our own hands. It's important that we wait on God and His timing as we seek to live for Him.

Jesus is a perfect example of this.

Travel with me in your mind to a desert wilderness. It's hot. It's empty. It's lonely. Jesus willingly hid Himself away there for forty days and nights to pray. In Matthew 4:1–11 we read about how Jesus sought the face of His Father and faced down the temptations of the Enemy.

In between verse 11 and verse 12, my Bible adds this little notation: "Jesus Begins His Ministry."

First Jesus sought God; then Jesus served. He came out of the wilderness ready to do kingdom work. "From that time Jesus began to preach, saying, 'Repent, for the kingdom of heaven is at hand'" (Matthew 4:17).

Jesus waited to hear from His Father before He did any kingdom work. He didn't take matters into His own hands. He didn't move based on what He already knew about how God works. He prayed. He listened to God. He waited for specific instructions from mission control.

The disciples did the same thing. Acts 1 picks up their story after Jesus' death and resurrection. He gives His disciples a very specific mission: "But you will receive power when the Holy Spirit has come upon you and you will be my witnesses in Jerusalem and in all Judea and Samaria, and to the end of the earth" (Acts 1:8).

How's that for a calling? Jesus tells the disciples their mission is to tell others about Him. They had seen Him die on the cross. They had seen Him rise from the dead. He had just spent forty days with them gearing them up for their mission. They heard their assignment straight from Jesus' mouth, and then they watched Him return to heaven in one last show of power.

And then Jesus' followers waited. They didn't jump up and run off to take the world by storm. They waited on God to give them the green light. Acts 2 tells us that they did not preach a single sermon or plant a single church until God sent the Holy Spirit to help them.

God wants to use you, but just like 007 waits for orders from his mysterious boss, "M," living on mission means you're not the one calling the shots. It requires you to be ready to move when God calls you but to willingly wait for His timing.

Pick Me, Pick Me

God uses all kinds of people in His Word to carry out His mission, but they all had one thing in common—a willingness to obey.

This reminds me of the calling of the prophet Isaiah. We don't know much about Isaiah except that God called him to point out sin, preach the good news, and share God's plan with the people of Israel. Isaiah 6 records Isaiah's vision of God in heaven. Isaiah wrote, "And I heard the voice of the Lord saying, 'Whom shall I send, and who will go for us?' Then I said, 'Here I am! Send me'" (Isaiah 6:8).

Those five words, "Here I am! Send me," are jam-packed with meaning. Isaiah was telling God, "Pick me! Pick me! I will go."

If we want to live on mission, we need to have Isaiah's attitude. We need to be willing to go where God wants us to go, to do what God wants us to do, and to move when

God calls us to move. That willing attitude includes having a heart open to whatever assignment God might have for you.

Do you want to make a difference? Do you want to be used by God to do something big? You don't have to make it happen or worry that you're not the kind of person God wants to use. If He can use a shepherd to deliver His people and a Jewish teenager to deliver the Messiah, He can use you! But you do have to be willing to follow God wherever He leads.

With that attitude in mind,
let's repeat Isaiah's words together:

"Here I am! Send me."

CHAPTER 4

You're
a Loser

magine you wake up one morning to find an envelope mysteriously placed on your bedroom dresser. You open it up and read the following:

> There's a girl in your second period math class who is really lonely. You've never noticed her (neither has anyone else), but I notice her. I know she feels friendless and hopeless. I know there are moments when she wonders if life is even worth living. I want you to be My hands and feet to that girl today. I want you to walk right up to her, look her in the eye, and talk to her. And I want you to invite her to come and hear about My love for her. This is your mission for today.
>
> WARNING: THIS MESSAGE WILL SELF-DESTRUCT
>
> Love,
> God

I realize that God doesn't leave mysterious mission messages in envelopes on our dressers. I am also aware that the self-destructive message shtick is more *Mission Impossible* than God-of-the-universe-type stuff. But bear with me.

You slide the message back in the envelope and consider your options. 1) You can pretend you never saw the envelope. 2) You can choose not to carry out your mission, making excuses to avoid Lonely Girl or math class altogether. 3) You can say, "Yes, Lord" and show Lonely Girl God's love.

Before you make your choice, you should pull that mission back out of the envelope and read the fine print. I guarantee there will be fine print, because living on mission always has risks. There is no such thing as a God-sized mission that starts and ends with a stroll down Easy Street. In fact, if we see saying yes to mission-minded living like walking down a path or a road, we should look carefully for the sign that will most surely read, "Warning: Loss ahead!"

Let's use talking to Lonely Girl as an example. What are the risks? Just because God calls you to talk to her doesn't mean Lonely Girl will talk back. There is a real risk of rejection with this mission. What if she does talk? What if she opens right up about feeling depressed and lonely? What then? Do you know what to say to her? Do you know what Bible verses to give her? There's a risk you'll screw it up. Lonely Girl is probably lonely for a reason. You don't become a social outcast by being the most beautiful, talented, outgoing gal in the school. She might be weird. She might be so glad she has someone to talk to that she thinks you are instant best friends. What then? What will people say when you are the new BFF of the weirdest girl in math class? There is a risk of being made fun of or at the very least, misunderstood.

Rejection. Failure. Being made fun of. These are the risks of obeying God in the little task of talking to someone. I don't want to sugarcoat saying yes to God. Often, the bigger the task, the higher the stakes.

✿ I'm a Loser

Remember when I felt God was asking me to give up my teaching job to write about Him to young women? I felt like a total loser during that season, mostly because I was.

I lost the career I had spent years building. I had to give up the security of knowing what my life would look like. I lost a steady paycheck. Peanut butter and jelly sandwiches and Ramen noodles are fine for a season, but I was kind of hoping a college degree would afford me fine dining options like Velveeta Shells and Cheese. Obeying God meant giving up having enough money to be as comfortable as I'd like to be. Then there was my reputation. I walked into my boss's office one day and said, "I need to resign." He asked me why. I said I had no idea. He asked me where I would work. I said I had no leads. I worried this would make me sound like a crazy person, and apparently it did. When word got around that I was quitting for no good reason, I got plenty of weird looks.

I understand that the risks of quitting a job may not exactly matter to you. You're probably not in the stage of life when a job is super important. But what if God asked you to give up something that did matter to you? An athletic scholarship? A spot on the swim team? A relationship with a guy you're in love with? What if the mission God has for you doesn't make sense

to your friends and makes you stick out from the crowd like a sore thumb? What if it means tossing out something you've worked really hard for?

What then? When there is risk involved with living on mission (and there always is), do you still want to let God use you?

Let's backtrack to Moses and Mary. For them, living on mission came at a high cost. Moses had to push through a speech impediment, persuade a powerful and stubborn Pharaoh, and lead a grouchy group of people for more than four decades. The angel Gabriel seemed to skirt out of town about the time Mary had to tell her momma and her fiancé that a baby was coming and ask them to believe her purity was still intact. Then she had to carry that baby for nine long months, deliver Him in a stable, and love Him all the way to the cross. Saying yes to God's specific calling cost Mary and Moses all of those shallow wells they might have looked to before to give their lives meaning including comfort, achievement, and popularity. Saying yes to God when He called me to write meant giving up a career I had spent many years working toward, a steady paycheck, the approval of friends and coworkers, and a life that fit into a neat little box.

✿ Learning from Elisha's Calling

In 1 Kings 19:19–21 we find a little story jam-packed with truth about what it means to live with purpose. With talk of oxen and cloaks, the context may seem a little odd, but stick with me as I introduce one of my favorite losers of all time, Elisha.

> So [Elijah] departed from there and found Elisha the son of Shaphat, who was plowing with twelve yoke of oxen in front of him, and he was with the twelfth. Elijah passed by him and cast his cloak upon him. And he left the oxen and ran after Elijah and said, "Let me kiss my father and my mother, and then I will follow you." And he said to him, "Go back again, for what have I done to you?" And he returned from following him and took the yoke of oxen and sacrificed them and boiled their flesh with the yokes of the oxen and gave it to the people, and they ate. Then he arose and went after Elijah and assisted him.

Here's the backstory: Elijah was a powerful prophet whom God used to clean up the land of Israel by kicking out false Gods. Elijah's mission was to call people back to pure worship of God. In 1 Kings 19, Elijah had a little breakdown. He got super stressed because living on mission cost him a lot. In fact, the leaders of the nation wanted to kill him because of his preaching. Elijah vented about all of this to God, and God responded by giving Elijah instructions to anoint Elisha as his successor. That's where we pick things up in verse 19. Elijah finds Elisha in the field, he puts his cloak on him as a sign of taking him under his wing as an apprentice of sorts, and just like that Elisha's mission becomes very, very clear.

Let's pick the story apart so we can learn.

Elisha was out plowing his field (reminds me of Moses and the sheep).

Like the others we've looked at, Elisha waited for God to call him to a very specific assignment.

And when that calling came, what was Elisha's response?

"Let me kiss my father and mother and then I will follow you." Then he destroyed the oxen and headed off into a whole new life singularly focused on serving the Lord (1 Kings 19:20).

♡ "Yes, Lord!"

♡

◁

Elisha didn't hesitate. He didn't play twenty questions with Elijah to make sure everything would work out according to his plan. He didn't do a risk assessment. He kissed his old life goodbye and watched it burn. He let his feet say "Yes, Lord!"

Elisha was a total loser. He lost (gave up) everything he loved to follow God. But Elisha is not the only loser in the Bible.

Genesis 12:1–2 records how Abram (God later changed his name to Abraham) hears the calling of God: "Now the Lord said to Abram, 'Go from your country and your kindred and your father's house to the land that I will show you. And I will make of you a great nation, and I will bless you and make your name great, so that you will be a blessing.'"

Abram's calling was BIG. God wanted to use him to build a nation, but it was gonna cost him. God asked Abram to give up his home, his family, and his familiar territory. The second wave of sacrifices meant Abram had to give up his security and comfort. Telling God "Yes, Lord" cost Abram almost everything.

How about Noah? God gave him a specific assignment, right? Does that make him a loser? "And God said to Noah, 'I have determined to make an end of all flesh, for the earth is filled with violence through them. Behold, I will destroy them with the earth. Make yourself an ark of gopher wood. Make rooms in the ark, and cover it inside and out with pitch'" (Genesis 6:13–14).

God had a big plan. He was going to wipe out everything on the earth and start over. Noah was part of that plan. Noah's mission was to build a big boat.

I'm sure that boat was expensive. God didn't give Noah a stack of cash to purchase supplies, so obedience likely tapped Noah's bank account. Building a giant ark probably also forced some losses in the relationship department. Noah's mission didn't make a lick of sense to anyone until after it started raining. I'm sure plenty of folks stood around with their fingers in an L on their foreheads to call Noah a loser, and he was. He gave up a lot to live on mission.

But Noah weighed the cost and still said, "Yes, Lord": "Noah did everything just as God commanded him" (Genesis 6:22 NIV).

The disciples were losers too. When Jesus called the twelve to work with Him, He also asked them to lose a few things. They walked away from their

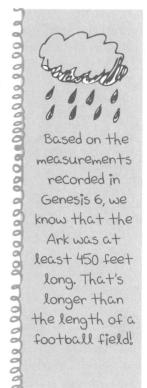

Based on the measurements recorded in Genesis 6, we know that the Ark was at least 450 feet long. That's longer than the length of a football field!

fishing boats and medical practices, at least temporarily. They lost the approval of others, as they were chased out of town after town where they preached. Eventually, almost all of them died as a result of their faith in Christ.

Is living on mission starting to sound a little scary? Does the reality that saying "Yes, Lord" has cost people their reputation, their security, and even their lives make you want to rethink pursuing your God-given purpose?

You are not alone. Remember the girls in the Gallery? Fear of loss was the number one thing that kept them from putting God's purposes above their own.

The girls told us they felt peer pressure not to be passionate and they feared there would be backlash from their friends if they agreed to let God use them for something big. They also said they were afraid of being bullied for standing up for God's Truth. They had this idea that living out their purpose would somehow get easier when they got older and that tools like college degrees would somehow minimize the risks.

Certainly fear of rejection and bullying are legitimate, but should those fears keep you frozen, unwilling to take a risk for Jesus' sake? Not if you want God to use you. Not if you want Him to accomplish His purposes for your life. Not if you want to be involved in something big.

❀ Loss of Life

We have this idea that God will never call us to hard things or that if something doesn't feel good, it must not be of God. That's just bad theology. The Bible shoots straight and tells us that living our lives for Christ will cost us.

Jesus says, "Whoever finds his life will lose it, and whoever loses his life for my sake will find it" (Matthew 10:39).

Unlike the disciples, you will probably never be martyred for the cause of Christ, so what is Jesus talking about as it applies to you? What does it mean to lose your life?

Jesus is unlocking a great mystery. If we get a death grip on our lives—on the things we love and value and want—we will find it all slipping through our fingers. Life is fragile and unpredictable, and we simply do not have enough control to make sure everything goes exactly according to plan. But Jesus flips it. (He does that a lot.) He says that if we want to hold on to our lives, we have to let go. We have to give up control and let Him be in charge. We have to loosen our grip on our own plans and let Him take the wheel. When we do, He doesn't just give us our lives back. He offers us a brand-new option: of trading in our old self-focused lives for brand-new lives focused on Him. It's a trade up.

Theology simply means the study of God.

❀ Count the Cost

Jesus doesn't trick us into a mission. In fact, He warns us to consider our losses before we ever say yes to His assignment.

> For which of you, desiring to build a tower, does not first sit down and count the cost, whether he has enough to complete it? Otherwise, when he has laid a foundation and is not able to finish, all who see it

begin to mock him, saying, "This man began to build and was not able to finish." Or what king, going out to encounter another king in war, will not sit down first and deliberate whether he is able with ten thousand to meet him who comes against him with twenty thousand? And if not, while the other is yet a great way off, he sends a delegation and asks for terms of peace. So therefore, any one of you who does not renounce all that he has cannot be my disciple. (Luke 14:28–33)

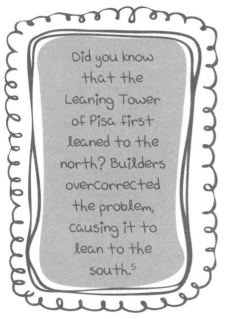

Did you know that the Leaning Tower of Pisa first leaned to the north? Builders overcorrected the problem, causing it to lean to the south.[5]

Jesus draws great word pictures. In this passage He gives us two examples to wrap our minds around. The first is a builder who is commissioned to build a tower. Jesus asks if the builder would go out and just start hammering some boards together without a plan. The answer is no, of course. Otherwise the builder might end up with his own Leaning Tower of Pisa or worse, no tower at all.

Next Jesus talks about a king. Imagine a king who decides to make war on a neighboring kingdom without thinking it through. What if he took only one hundred soldiers and then got to the battlefield and found his enemy had brought an army of 100,000? Failure to count the cost would cost him the war.

Then Jesus delivers this blow: "So therefore, any one of you who does not renounce all that he has cannot be my disciple" (Luke 14:33).

What does Jesus mean when He says that if we don't renounce everything we have we cannot be His disciples? Does He mean everything? As in *everything* everything?

Before you start thinking about stuff you don't want to give up, I want you to know that Jesus is most interested in your heart. This passage is about a willingness to lose. It's about a willingness to make sacrifices to be used by God.

God is good. He is not going to take things away from you just to watch you squirm. But if you want to be His disciple, if you want to be used by Him, Jesus wants you to know there will be a cost.

❀ This Isn't Bungee Jumping

Living on mission is not the same as signing up for an adventurous vacation. True, it is exciting to live for God and to be used in His big story, but it comes at a cost. A cost may seem look like a dark cloud, but there is a silver lining.

1 Thessalonians 5:24 says,
"He who calls you is faithful; he will surely do it."

You see, God didn't need Moses. He could have simply beamed the people of Israel into the Promised Land if He'd wanted to. He didn't need

Mary either. He could have arrived as a man, ready to reign. He doesn't need us to accomplish His purposes. He *chooses* to use us because it delights Him.

If God calls you to a mission, it is important that you respond with a yes, but you also need to know that the outcome does not rest on your shoulders.

The outcome rests squarely on the big shoulders of God. If He calls you to something, you can know for sure He will be faithful to carry you through the tough stuff. If necessary, He will carry you across the finish line.

Philippians 1:6 promises, "And I am sure of this, that he who began a good work in you will bring it to completion at the day of Jesus Christ."

God-sized missions often look impossible. Getting the people of Israel out of Egypt and into the Promised Land was not a walk in the park. Neither was delivering God's Son in a barn. God called Esther to ask the king to save her people. She risked her life to do it. He called Joshua to fight a huge military battle using only trumpets. It didn't make sense and the stakes were sky-high if he failed, but Joshua obeyed. He called Jonah to preach to his enemies in Nineveh. He called the disciples to drop their fishing nets and follow Him into a life they knew nothing about. He called Paul to start churches in hostile territory.

When God asks you to live your life on mission, you may feel like you're standing at the bottom of an Everest-sized mountain. But listen closely to what the angel told Mary when she was called to do something big for God:

60

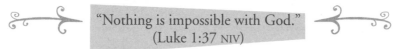

"Nothing is impossible with God."
(Luke 1:37 NIV)

When we read the stories of Moses, Mary, and others who received a very specific mission from God, we can be encouraged to know that God does all of the heavy lifting. You don't have to live on mission in your own strength. You do have to say yes to God, for whom nothing is impossible.

Sand Collecting

When I think about what I must lose in order to say, "Yes, Lord!" it reminds me of sand collecting. I once knew a woman with a huge collection of sand. She had bottles of sand from every beach you can imagine. Black sand, pink sand, white sand, and golden sand all sat in tiny jars around her house. But there was a catch: The woman had never been outside of her landlocked home state, smack dab in the middle of the USA. She had never even seen the ocean with her own eyes. The risks of traveling seemed too great, so she was content to look at sand through a glass jar.

If you've been to the ocean, you know the experience can't compare to looking at a little jar of sand. It may cost you something to get there, but the benefits of digging your toes into the sand and experiencing the vast ocean God created is worth it.

A sideline mentality says, "I can't do something big for God because there is risk." But when we refuse to let God use us, it's like keeping sand in a jar. We miss out on something so big and so powerful that we haven't really avoided losing at all.

CHAPTER 5

Purpose
stories

irst Timothy 4:12 reads, "Let no one despise you for your youth, but set the believers an example in speech, in conduct, in love, in faith, in purity."

These words were written from the apostle Paul to a young man named Timothy, who was a leader in a church Paul started. First Timothy is a little book with big ideas—like what it means to be shaped by the gospel and how to deal with false teachers. In the midst of all of that heavy stuff, this little gem of a verse glimmers and grabs our attention. Paul is telling Timothy he doesn't have to sit on the sidelines just because he's young. In fact, Paul encourages Timothy to set the bar for others in the church in the areas of speech, conduct, love, faith, and purity.

Turn that verse over in your mind a few times, and this pearl will emerge—just because you're young doesn't mean you can't do big things with your life. In fact, God's Word calls you to set an example for others, including those who are older than you.

I wonder why Paul felt the need to write those words to Timothy. Maybe Timothy was getting some pushback from the older folks in his church for boldly leading them to look more like Jesus.

Remember the girls in the Gallery? They felt pushback too. When they stepped out of their comfort zone to do something big for God, it seemed like adults took all of the credit or their peers made fun of them. It's not fun to feel undervalued or ridiculed, but Paul's words to Timothy can make a difference in how we respond.

Paul urged Timothy to live in such a way that others could not look down their noses at him. He asked Timothy to do such big things with his faith that others would have no choice but to look up.

I'd like to give you the exact same challenge.

Do something now! Don't wait until you're older or have your ducks all lined up in a neat little row to be willing to be used by God. It doesn't matter how old you are; you can set an example for believers of all ages and stations in life. You can show them what it looks like to live on mission. You can let God use you for something so big that others look up to you and ultimately see Him.

Don't believe me? Check out these stories of real people just like you who are doing big things for Jesus before they even graduate from high school.

Madison Learns to Hug a Bear, Not a Boy

Madison was just a normal thirteen-year-old girl when God gave her a big assignment. She went on a mission trip where she heard God's Truth about purity. She committed to save her heart and her body for her husband, but it didn't feel like enough. God used that trip to light a fire in her heart to share the importance of purity with other girls. But how would she do that? She wasn't a speaker like the one she'd heard on the mission trip. She didn't have opportunities to talk to thousands of students about staying pure. She didn't have a website or a book deal or a platform. She was just a girl who happened to still have math homework. What could she do to spread God's Truth about purity?

The idea hit her all at once. A bear. What if she found a way to encourage her friends to hug a bear and not a boy?

So she called up seven friends and invited them to the mall. They each bought a bear and then gathered at a table in the food court. They wrote letters to their future husbands and put them inside the bear, they prayed for each other to remain pure, and they promised to hold each other accountable.

Find out more about Madison's mission at boyfriendbears.org.

Madison had been faithful to say, "Yes, Lord!" but God was not done with her. He called her and her friends to begin speaking to other girls in their community about purity. They wanted to give every girl who heard their message a bear as a tool to help them wait. The boyfriend bear was born.

Madison is now fifteen and managing a ministry that allows her to speak about purity to girls across the nation. Hundreds of girls now have a boyfriend bear to hold as an alternative to romantic relationships outside of God's timing. Has she set an example for other believers in the area of purity? You betcha.

Madison told me she has been made fun of for taking a stand and that responding to God's calling hasn't always been easy. But she says it's worth it. She wouldn't trade living on mission for living life as a "normal" teenager for anything.

Carolina Loves on the Lonely

Carolina received her calling straight from God's Word.

Matthew 25:35–36 says, "For I was hungry and you gave me food, I was thirsty and you gave me drink, I was a stranger and you welcomed me, I was naked and you clothed me, I was sick and you visited me, I was in prison and you came to me."

Carolina wondered what would happen if she took this verse literally. Could she make a difference if she worked to feed, love, and visit those who were in need?

For her senior project at a Christian high school, Carolina decided to put this verse into action. She titled her project, "Will This Loneliness Ever End?" Her goal was simple. She just wanted to help others in need.

Once a month she visited people living in trailer parks to share her testimony. Carolina says, "Visiting the people who live in trailer parks was a great experience I will never forget. I had the chance to meet so many amazing people I never would have met without my project. On the other hand, it was really sad to meet so many people who are going through a lot of difficult circumstances in their lives and don't have anyone to help them."

Carolina also launched an initiative in her hometown called One warm Coat. She asked people in her church and school to provide warm clothes for the needy. She delivered those items to homeless people she found on the street during a special trip to New York City. "The trip to New York was amazing," says Carolina. "I got to spend time with people who were in need of everything and who didn't know God. It was really nice to help the people we found sleeping on the street in the cold and snowy weather by giving them coats."

God had already done some big things with Carolina, but He wasn't finished. Carolina kept saying, "Yes, Lord" as He prompted her to meet others' needs. She planned an event to raise money for the orphanage in the Dominican Republic where she grew up. That event raised $5,000, which the orphanage used to feed and clothe the children in their care, says Carolina.

Carolina shared her life story with me, including her many years in an orphanage where workers took care of her and told her about God's love. Her passion to give back to the people who had given so much to her kept her motivated as she worked to raise funds.

Carolina's mission reminds me of a challenge God gives to all of us. James 1:22 says, "But be doers of the word, and not hearers only, deceiving yourselves."

God asks us to do more than just read our Bibles. His assignment is not for us to listen to sermon after sermon, Bible study after Bible study, soaking in God's Word like a sponge but never doing anything with it. The Bible should prompt us to move.

Carolina didn't hear God speak from a burning bush. Instead she simply read the Bible and decided to do what it says.

❀ Asbury Asks Hard Questions

During our research for this book, we found a youth group in Asbury, Oklahoma, where living on mission is a big deal. The youth pastors have a chosen theme they pound into their students' heads: "Junior high students can change the world." They are intentional about teaching students the same principle Paul taught Timothy: that God wants to use them right now, even though they're young. The youth pastors told us that many of their students felt the first tug on their hearts to live on mission in middle school. The leaders simply responded by saying, "Don't wait. Go for it!"

The results have been amazing.

★ Geneva organized a project called "Loose Change to Loosen Chains." She raised more than $500 for the International Justice Mission, an organization that rescues victims of violence, sexual exploitation, slavery, and oppression.

★ Mallory raised $350 by working in her neighborhood all summer babysitting, raking leaves, etc. She donated every cent to charity.

⭐ Meghan wrote letters to her teachers asking them to donate toward International Justice Mission. Many teachers gave donations.

⭐ One group of students made $600 selling bracelets. They gave it all away to fund ministry.

⭐ One student organized a community-wide water balloon fight to raise awareness and funds for those in need.

The Asbury youth pastors told us that completing these short-term assignments often merged into long-term commitments. Once students were bit with the bug to serve others and to live on mission, they wanted to do more. Many of them now lead small groups, teach others, or volunteer in other ministries of the church.

✿ Lexi Writes for Hope

Lexi's calling sounds a lot like mine. God asked her to use words to make a difference.

Lexi was living like any ordinary teenager when God spoke to her heart about orphans in India. She single-handedly developed a character-based Bible curriculum with the goal of teaching moral values and basic concepts of risk and safety. She wrote with young Indian girls in mind, especially those who are at risk of being sold as slaves. Lexi used God's Word to teach about forgiveness and self-respect to girls half a world away. When she finished, she put the curriculum into the hands of a missionary. It is now being taught to children in villages and schools in Rajasthan, India. Lexi had plenty of opportunities to say, "Yes, Lord," but there would be even more.

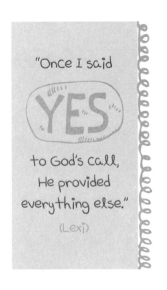

"Once I said YES to God's call, He provided everything else."

(Lexi)

In April of Lexi's senior year of high school, her missionary friend in India invited her to come and teach the curriculum. Lexi would have to travel around the globe alone, immerse herself in a foreign culture, and look into the eyes of a group of girls who might spend their lives as slaves. Still, Lexi said, "Yes."

In India, Lexi taught her curriculum to children at a brothel and got to see the beginning of the rescue home being built with money she helped raise. Then she hopped back on the plane and came home in time for finals.

Lexi didn't wait. When she saw the collision of a need and an opportunity, Lexi stepped up to the plate. "When I felt God calling me to do this project, I was tentative about it," Lexi admits. "It seemed like I was biting off more than I could chew. I was afraid of failing, but I took the leap of faith. What I found was that the success of the campaign didn't depend on me at all—it was all on God. Once I said yes to His call, He provided everything else. He opened all the doors, and He gave my efforts the momentum they needed to succeed. My job was simply to say yes."

These are big things by any standard, but let me make one thing clear: God often calls us to assignments that our human hearts might measure as small. For example, God calls you to love your neighbors—and that includes your siblings. I have four brothers and sisters, so I happen to know that this is a particularly difficult mission (harder than writing books!). He might call you to do something that no one (other than God) will ever notice. He might ask you to do something that seems small and meaningless for someone who is difficult to minister to.

I don't want to give you the impressions that saying "Yes, Lord" will necessarily mean becoming a published author or the leader of a ministry or a missionary to a foreign land. He might do any of those things in your life, but I would hate for you to devalue the small faithfulnesses God may be calling you to: obey your parents respectfully, limit your screen time, or befriend the friendless girl. Those things seem small, but they are not small to God!

Where Do I Start?

These stories are inspiring. They are proof that it's possible to do something big for God at any age. They remind me of times in my own life when God called and I answered yes. I am so thankful for every opportunity God has given me to make a difference in His kingdom.

But these stories also remind me of the times when I've said no. Times when God has asked me to move or change or step up and I have let excuses get the best of me. I hate to think of what I missed out on.

You are at a fork in the road. When you read the last word and close this book, you will have a choice to make. Will you live your life on mission? Will you count the cost, knowing that serving God might make you a loser, and still choose to say, "Yes, Lord"? Or will you miss the boat and decide to watch from shore as others allow God to use them to accomplish big things?

I hope you'll chose the first option, but that may have you wondering, "How do I start?" Here are a few questions to help with that.

What Am I Passionate About?

I told you in the first chapter of this book that I have a theory. Some of our passions are a result of our experiences and our environment, but there are other passions—the ones that really light a fire in our bellies— that God places in our hearts to prepare us to live on mission.

One great place to start to live on mission is by simply asking yourself, "What am I passionate about?" Then ask God to shape those passions into an assignment that will bring Him glory.

✿ What Is My Mess?

I realize I've beaten you over the head with the idea that you might be called to do something with a God-given passion, but passion isn't the only way to zero in on a calling. As we study people who have lived on mission, another pattern emerges. Often their mission was connected to a failure or loss.

If you read the first book in this series, *My Name Is Erin: One Girl's Journey to Discover Truth*, you know Aly's story. Aly is a Christian. She's a straight-A student. She has always been involved in her church. But two years ago Aly was living a double life. She was dating a non-Christian behind her parents' backs. The relationship turned sexual. This led her to make other compromises, including using drugs and alcohol. She hid her sin for months, but eventually the truth came out.

Aly had to endure a painful process of repentance and making things right, but as she did, God did something amazing. He gave her opportunities to share her struggles with other teenagers who needed to hear that they could experience forgiveness for their secret sins. When I asked Aly if I could write about her story, she said, "If one girl chooses God's Truth because of my story it would all be worth it to me."

God took Aly's mess and turned it into a message about His forgiveness. ♡ ♡

One of the girls from the Gallery has a dad with ALS, a devastating disease that causes loss of muscle control. Watching her dad suffer is painful for her, but when the conversation turned to purpose she said she has a feeling that her dad's disease will play a role. She believes God will use this messy part of her life to accomplish something big.

It shouldn't surprise us when God works this way. In His Word He promises us that He will. Romans 8:28 says, "And we know that for those who love God all things work together for good, for those who are called according to his purpose."

God has a plan for you, and there's nothing in your life that He can't use.

I have a good friend who was going through a difficult season in life when she sensed that God had an odd assignment for her. She felt Him nudging her to use only what was in her pantry as she cooked for the next several weeks. She came up with some "interesting" culinary creations, but as she did she felt God teaching her that He could use everything in her life, even the yucky stuff, for His glory.

Are there parts of your life that are messy? How about an area of past sin? Have you experienced pain, trials, or heartbreak? These are the areas of your life you may be tempted to toss out with the trash, but God wants to use them.

In 2 Corinthians 1:3–4 we read, "Blessed be the God and Father of our Lord Jesus Christ, the Father of mercies and God of all comfort, who comforts us in all our affliction, so that we may be able to comfort those who are in any affliction, with the comfort with which we ourselves are comforted by God."

God comforts us. We comfort others. It's a simple mission, but one you can accept right now. Wanna start living on mission today? Find someone who is going through something you've been through and find a way to comfort that person.

Be a Doer

Remember Carolina? She discovered her purpose simply by doing what she read in the Bible. Living out God's Word is a fantastic way to live on mission. If you don't know where to start, begin by reading God's Word often and asking God to show you how you can put what you read into action.

Take the Leap

I told you that living on mission is not exactly the same as taking an adventure vacation. It's not bungee jumping, but it does require a leap—specifically a leap of faith that God will keep His promises to be strong when you are weak and to finish what He starts in you.

You don't have to drum up a calling. You don't have to spend years studying and preparing to be used by God. You don't have to wait until you are older, wiser, or richer to make a difference in God's kingdom. Now is the perfect time to get off the sidelines and get into the game of what God is doing.

Why did God make me? is a very good question. *I don't know* is not a very good answer. His Word says that you were made to give God glory. Your purpose on the planet is to make Him famous.

For me that looks like teaching God's Truth to young women like you through writing and speaking. It's not the life I had planned for myself, but living on mission, focused on pursuing my God-given purpose is the best ride I've ever been on. I wouldn't trade it for all of the shallow wells in the world.

God has a plan for your life. When you say yes to the script He has written for you, that's when the real story begins.

My name is

_____,

and this is my story.

[write in your name here]

For I know the plans I have for you, declares the Lord, plans to prosper you and not to harm you, plans to give you hope and a future.
Jeremiah 29:11

NOTES

1. Erin Davis, *My Name is Erin: One Girl's Journey to Discover Who She Is* (Chicago: Moody Publishers, 2013), 33.

2. Steven P. Marsh, "Meet Milly, Possibly the Puniest Pooch in the World," *New York Daily News,* April 6, 2012. www.nydailynews.com.

3. Tamar Love Grande, "10 Weirdest Beauty Rituals from Around the World," Smosh.com, November 29, 2010. www.smosh.com.

4. Erin Davis, *My Name Is Erin: One Girl's Journey to Discover Truth* (Chicago: Moody Publishers, 2013), 55.

5. Nova, "History of Inventions: Fall of the Leaning Tower," Nova Online, November 2000. www.pbs.org.

Acknowledgments

My momma taught me better than to receive a gift without sending a thank-you note. This series is the end result of many gifts—people who love me well, friends who cheer me on, and fellow Jesus-lovers who consistently point me toward God's Truth. If you fit into one (or all) of those three camps, this page is my thank-you note to you. (Be sure to mention to my mom that I sent it!)

The Gab Gallery. I loved the girls I met during the research phase of this book. Your openness and honesty helped me know what to write. You also encouraged and inspired me by proving my suspicions that God is using young women to do big things. Keep letting Him use you. I'm on the edge of my seat waiting to see what mountains God will move with your generation. I did not get to meet all of you personally; instead some of you had the treat of hanging out with my friend, Dree. Speaking of . . .

Dree. Dree was my focus-group leader for the book. She hung out with girls in places like Little Rock, Springfield, and Tulsa. Anyone who had the chance to spend time with Dree knows what a treasure she is. Dree, I credit you with giving me the Truth bug. Your passion for God and His Word is positively infectious. Thanks for consistently pressing me to choose God's Truth and to live my life according to His Word. If we were back in junior high, I'd want you to wear the other half of my BFF necklace.

Holly, René, and Team Moody. I am so thankful for a publishing team who believes in the message of God's Truth and entrusts me to deliver that message to young women. Your kindness bowls me over. Thank you.

Jason, Eli, and Noble. At the end of the day, I am Jason's wife and Eli's and Noble's mom. These are the roles that bring me the most joy and force me to keep running to God's Word for answers. My sweet family listened to endless readings as this work evolved from an idea into a four-book series. When the process got stressful, they did things like make me a leaf pile and invite me to jump in. Family, I adore you. You are the very best part of my story.

Jesus. Thank You, Jesus, for being so completely irresistible.

Also available as ebooks

MOODY
PUBLISHERS

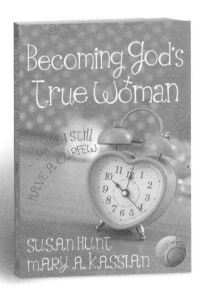

Becoming God's True Woman

Who did God make you to be? What kind of person will you become? What does God's word say about things like beauty, friendships, guys, and dating?

Also available as an ebook

MOODY
PUBLISHERS

978-0-8024-0360-5